Before Brother knew it, Bonnie had the dance floor. A huge crowd of cubs made a circle around them. They were clapping and shouting, "Brother's gotta dance! Brother's gotta dance!"

Then the music started, and Bonnie was dancing like crazy. Brother tried to pick up the beat, BUT HE COULDN'T MOVE HIS FEET! They were stuck to the floor! The music pounded in his ears. The crowd shouted, "Gotta dance! Gotta dance!"

BIG CHAPTER BOOKS

The Berenstain Bears and the Drug Free Zone

The Berenstain Bears and the New Girl in Town

The Berenstain Bears Gotta Dance!

The Berenstain Bears and the Nerdy Nephew

The Berenstain Bears Accept No Substitutes

The Berenstain Bears and the Female Fullback

The Berenstain Bears and the Red-Handed Thief

The Berenstain Bears
and the Wheelchair Commando

The Berenstain Bears and the School Scandal Sheet

The Berenstain Bears and the Galloping Ghost

The Berenstain Bears at Camp Crush

The Berenstain Bears and the Giddy Grandma

The Berenstain Bears and the Dress Code

Coming soon

The Berenstain Bears' Media Madness

The Berenstain Bears in the Freaky Funhouse

The Berenstain Bears GOTTA DANCE!

by Stan & Jan Berenstain

A BIG CHAPTER BOOK™

Random House 🏠 New York

Library of Congress Cataloging-in-Publication Data
Berenstain, Stan.
The Berenstain Bears gotta dance / by Stan & Jan Berenstain.
        p.   cm. — (A Big chapter book)
SUMMARY: With the help of Sister's ballet teacher, Brother Bear
conquers his fear of dancing and can ask his favorite girl cub to
the school dance.
ISBN 0-679-84032-X (pbk.) — ISBN 0-679-94032-4 (lib. bdg.)
[1. Dancing—Fiction. 2. Ballet dancing—Fiction. 3. Bears—
Fiction. 4. Brothers and sisters—Fiction.] I. Berenstain, Jan. II.
Title. III. Title: Berenstain Bears gotta dance. IV. Series:
Berenstain, Stan.   Big chapter book.
PZ7.B4483Berf   1993   92-32565
[Fic]—dc20

Contents

Chapter 1
Brother's Big Problem

The smell of flowers and new leaves filled
the air as Brother and Sister Bear walked
home from school. It was that time of year
when both softball and basketball are
played. Brother spent the whole walk home
telling Sister all about the base hits he had
made at morning recess and the baskets he
had sunk during afternoon recess.

Finally he ran out of things to brag about. So Sister changed the subject to something she found much more interesting.

"Did I tell you I'm going to a party at Lizzy Bruin's tonight?" she asked. "We'll be doing all the new steps. We'll dance till we drop!"

Brother made a face. "Great, Sis. Wiggle and jump around to dopey music all night. What a stupid thing to do."

Sister frowned. Why did Brother always make fun of dancing? Was it because she liked it so much? Sister tried to think of something mean to say about sports. But then she had an even better idea.

"Have you heard the rumor about Bonnie Brown?" she asked. "They say she's going to invite Too-Tall Grizzly to the Spring Dance!"

Brother didn't answer. He just stared straight ahead, looking very hurt.

Brother was surprised by his feelings. It wasn't as if he and Bonnie were boyfriend and girlfriend. But they had just played Romeo and Juliet in the spring play and had become very good friends. As for Too-Tall— how could she ask *him* to the dance? Bonnie thought Too-Tall was awful.

Sister could see that her news had hit home. Hmm, she thought. My dance-hating big brother has a real problem.

Brother did have a problem. Brother had been thinking about Bonnie a lot lately. He was even starting to feel that he would like to be more than just friends with Bonnie. He was starting to feel he would like to go out on dates with her. He wanted to go to the movies with her, to the Burger Bear, and to dances . . .

Dances. That was the real problem.

Brother had tried dancing at parties. But as soon as he got up and started wiggling, he felt silly. He felt as if the different parts of his body didn't know each other. He was afraid of being laughed at. And the more afraid he got, the worse he danced. There was no question about it—when it came to dancing, Brother was a real klutz.

So whenever anyone talked about dancing, Brother just made fun of it. Most

of the other cubs thought he was a real snob about dancing.

Not being able to dance wasn't all bad. It was a good excuse whenever some girl Brother didn't like very much—Babs Bruno, for example—asked him to go to a party. "Gee, Babs, I'd like to go," he would say. "But I don't know how to dance. I have two left feet."

But now with Bonnie on his mind, Brother's feelings about dancing were a problem. Bonnie Brown was a great dancer . . . and he was a dancing klutz. Why would she ever want to go steady with him? He was afraid to even step onto a dance floor!

Walking along, Brother felt sick. Would Bonnie really go to the dance with Too-Tall? Was the rumor true?

Brother was afraid that maybe it was true. Even though Too-Tall was a big jerk, Brother had to admit that he was a great dancer. Like Bonnie, Too-Tall knew all the latest steps. He knew the Grunge, the Bear Hug, the Slew-Foot, and the Stoop. He had even made up some of his own—the Swivel and the Snake.

Bonnie knew that Brother didn't like to dance. So it made sense that she wouldn't ask him to the dance. It also made sense that she would want to go to the dance—and with someone who could really dance. So why wouldn't she ask the best boy-cub dancer in Bear Country, Too-Tall Grizzly?

Chapter 2

The Dancing Lesson

By the time the cubs got home, Brother looked very unhappy. Sister felt a little sorry for him.

"Why don't you let me give you some dancing lessons?" said Sister.

That made Brother even more unhappy. Get help from his little sister? Never! "Are you kidding?" he said.

"Well, okay," Sister said. "If you don't mind giving up your girl to that jerk Too-Tall."

"She's not my girl!" said Brother. "Besides, if she wants to ask Too-Tall to the dance, let her. I couldn't care less. Dancing is stupid. It's the dumbest thing in the world. Anyone who does it is just plain dumb."

Papa, who was reading the newspaper in his easy chair, shook his head. There goes Brother making fun of dancing again, he thought.

"If you say so," said Sister. "But I can just see old Too-Tall doing the Swivel with Bonnie. And let me tell you," she said, pretending to see something awful, "it's not a pretty sight."

Brother wasn't looking for a fight. But he had had enough of Sister's teasing. He went after her. Sister giggled as Brother chased her around the sofa.

Papa had had enough, too. He jumped up from his chair. "Stop that!" he roared.

Brother stopped, but he didn't stop being angry. Sister threw herself onto the rug. She clapped a hand over her mouth to hide her giggles.

Papa looked down at Brother. His angry face relaxed. He hated to see Brother so unhappy about something as much fun as dancing. "Son," he said, "why don't you do yourself a favor and learn to dance? It's really not that hard, you know."

"Why should I?" said Brother. "Dancing is stupid. Only stupid cubs like to dance."

"That's just sour grapes, young fellow," said Papa. "Do you know what sour grapes are?"

"Sure," said Brother. "Sour grapes are grapes that are sour."

" 'Sour grapes' is what you call it when someone makes fun of something because he can't do it."

Papa went to the bookshelves, took down the *B* book from the encyclopedia set, and opened it to "Ballroom Dancing." "Ah, yes, here it is," he said. " 'The Box Step': the basic step of all dancing. Here, son, take a look at this picture."

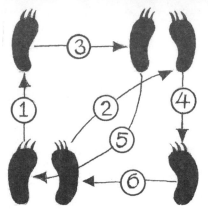

THE BOX STEP

"But Papa," said Sister, "the Box Step is prehistoric."

"He has to start somewhere," said Papa. He took hold of Brother's arm.

"You're just going to make things worse," said Sister. "The Box Step is to modern dancing what the doggie paddle is to the Australian crawl."

"Interesting point," said Papa. "But as I remember, both of you had to learn the doggie paddle before you could learn the Australian crawl."

Sister groaned and started to say, "It's not the same . . ." But she stopped. There was no point in arguing with Papa once he had his mind made up. And right then his mind was made up to teach Brother the old-fashioned Box Step.

"Let's have some music," said Papa. He turned on the radio and faced Brother. "All right, young man. I'm the girl, so take hold of me."

Brother tried to put his arms around Papa's wide body.

"Not like that!" cried Papa. "When you dance with a girl, you have to hold her like you mean it!"

"I'm trying, Papa," said Brother. "But I

can't reach around you."

"Like this!" said Papa. He grabbed Brother. Papa held him so close that he was almost smothered in Papa's big belly. Then he began to box-step him about the room.

"ONE-two-three-four," counted Papa. He moved his arm like a pump handle.

Sister hopped out of the way as Papa wheeled poor Brother around the room.

Mama came in from the kitchen. She looked at Papa and Brother with raised eyebrows.

"ONE-two-three-four, ONE-two-three-four," shouted Papa. "I'm teaching him the Box Step." He was pushing Brother around the living room the way a bulldozer might push a load of gravel around an unfinished parking lot.

Mama folded her arms and watched until

she had seen enough. "Let's stop nagging Brother about dancing," she said. "If he doesn't want to learn, *he doesn't have to.*"

Papa paid no attention. He kept on shoving poor Brother around the floor. "ONE-two-three-four, ONE-two-three . . ."

Sister hurried over to Mama. She whispered in her ear. "But he really wants to learn. He can't stand the idea of Bonnie asking Too-Tall to the Spring Dance."

"Is Bonnie going to do that?" Mama asked.

"That's the rumor," said Sister.

"I thought Too-Tall was going steady with Queenie," said Mama.

"That's an on-again, off-again thing," said Sister. "And right now it's off again."

Mama shook her head and sighed. "Let's drop it for now. Please set the table for dinner. Tomorrow is another day."

Chapter 3
Dance, Ballerina, Dance

Tomorrow was indeed another day. It was Saturday, the day Sister had ballet class.

This year Sister had fallen in love with ballet. And she had fallen hard. When she wasn't thinking about doing the Grunge, the Bear Hug, or the Slew-Foot at parties, she was thinking about ballet. She was thinking about first, second, and third positions. And she was thinking about all the other positions and movements she practiced every Saturday morning at Madame Bearishnikov's Ballet, Bearobics, and Fitness Center at the Bear Country Mall.

At breakfast that morning, Mama looked

up from her blueberry pancakes and said that she would not be able to take Sister to her ballet lessons as usual. "I'm going to give that job to you, Brother," she added.

"Aw, Mama," said Brother. "I was going to play softball with Cousin Freddy and—"

"No arguments, please," said Mama. "Sister is too young to go by herself. It's dangerous at the mall with cubs like Too-Tall and his gang hanging around."

Brother turned to Sister. "Has Too-Tall been bothering you?"

Sister made a face. "He and his gang hang around the Ballet Center and tease us. They do what they think are ballet positions. Then they yell, 'Look, Ma! I'm da-a-a-ancin'!'"

She popped a blueberry in her mouth and smiled. "But there's something else you should know. A certain Bonnie Brown

has started taking advanced classes with Madame Bearishnikov."

"Well, what are we waiting for?" said Brother. "Grab your jacket and let's go."

Before you could say "Brother loves Bonnie," Brother and Sister were on their way to the mall. Sister knew very well why Brother had changed his mind. He wanted to be near Bonnie. She also knew that Brother was always ready to protect his little sister against bullies like Too-Tall.

What she didn't know was that Brother

was thinking hard about his dancing problem. In fact, he had been thinking about it since yesterday. Last night he had even had a nightmare about dancing.

In the dream he was at the Spring Dance with Bonnie. She asked him to dance the Grunge with her. He tried to make excuses. First he had a sprained ankle, then an ingrown toenail. Finally he was sick to his stomach. But Bonnie wouldn't take "No" for an answer.

Before Brother knew it, Bonnie had him on the dance floor. A huge crowd of cubs made a circle around them. They were clapping and shouting, "Brother's gotta dance! Brother's gotta dance!"

Then the music started, and Bonnie was dancing like crazy. Brother tried to pick up the beat, BUT HE COULDN'T MOVE HIS

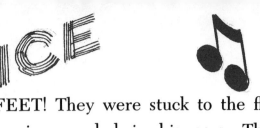

FEET! They were stuck to the floor! The music pounded in his ears. The crowd shouted, "Gotta dance! Gotta dance!"

Brother bent over and took hold of one leg and then the other, pulling with all his might. His feet came loose with a ripping sound. He looked down in horror. Big chunks of floor had come loose. They were stuck to his feet.

Suddenly Bonnie stopped dancing. She

looked at Brother as if he were the worst creep that ever lived. She turned and headed straight for somebody on the other side of the dance floor. Who was it? Brother tried to follow her, but the chunks of floor made it hard to walk. They went GLUMP-GLUMP-GLUMP as he walked along like some kind of Frankenstein monster. All he needed was a bolt through his neck.

Then Brother saw who Bonnie was

headed for. It was Too-Tall! They greeted each other like long-lost lovers. Now Too-Tall and Bonnie were dancing their brains out. The music was pounding. The crowd was screaming. All at once the crowd turned to poor Brother and broke into loud

screaming laughter.

Brother shuddered. Wow, what a nightmare! He would have to do *something* about his fear of dancing. Maybe he *could* learn, after all. But he was already so far behind the other cubs. There didn't seem to be any way he could catch up. He was sure he would make an awful fool of himself if he tried. He didn't know what to do.

"Hey, Sis," he said.

Sister looked up. She was a little surprised to hear Brother's voice. They were almost at the mall, and this was the first word Brother had spoken since they left the tree house.

"You know that . . . that Spring Dance thing?" asked Brother.

"What about it?" said Sister.

"You going to it?" said Brother.

"Of course," said Sister. "I wouldn't miss it for the world."

"Are . . . uh . . . a lot of cubs going?" Brother asked.

Sister laughed. "Are you kidding? Everyone who's anyone will be there. Everyone except my dopey stubborn brother."

"You think I'm stubborn, huh?"

"Stubborn, stubborn, *stub-bor-in!*"

Brother looked away. He kicked a stone by the side of the road. "Who are you going with?" he asked.

"Freddy," said Sister.

"Freddy?" said Brother. "But Freddy's our *cousin!*"

They turned a corner. Sister saw the mall and began to walk faster. "I'm not going to *marry* him," she said. "I'm just going to *dance* with him."

Chapter 4
Mall Mischief

"Look, Ma! We're da-a-a-ancin'!"

Too-Tall Grizzly and his gang were jumping around in front of Madame Bearishnikov's Ballet, Bearobics, and Fitness Center. They were having a great time making fun of ballet.

Smirk did a clumsy ballet leap.

Skuzz went into a fast twirl and then pretended to throw up.

Too-Tall stood up on tiptoe and went running around in a circle with a sweet smile on his face. He fluttered his eyelashes.

The ballet students tried not to giggle as they slipped past the gang and into the Ballet Center.

As Bonnie Brown came walking toward the Center, Too-Tall waved his arms at the gang. "Cool it," he said. "Ms. Brown is under my personal protection."

He hurried to meet her. She looked very cute in her leotard and leg warmers. Too-Tall linked his arm in hers, and the two walked along together.

Bonnie looked up at him. "Too-Tall, why are you so good to me?" she asked, as if she didn't really mean it.

Too-Tall gave her a crooked grin. "Because you're nuts about me. You just don't know it yet."

"But what about Queenie? I thought that you and she were an item," said Bonnie.

"A *discontinued* item," said Too-Tall.

Bonnie smiled. She shook her head. "Too-Tall, you're impossible."

"I try to be, little lady. I try to be," said Too-Tall. Then Bonnie disappeared into the

Ballet Center. Too-Tall turned back to his gang. "Okay, back to work!" he said.

Vinnie, Skuzz, and Smirk started up again. "Look, Ma! We're da-a-a-ancin'!"

By now Brother and Sister had reached the Ballet Center. "Did you see that?" asked Sister. "Miss Bonnie having some private words with You-Know-Who."

"Yeah," said Brother. "I know who, but I don't care who. Who Bonnie talks to is up to her. She can talk to the man in the moon, for all I care."

As they got close to Too-Tall and his gang, Brother said to Sister, "All right, give me your hand."

"Ooh, I didn't know you cared," Sister teased.

"I just don't want you telling Mama that I didn't take good care of you," said Brother.

Brother was the only boy cub coming

to the Ballet Center that morning. When
Too-Tall saw him, his eyes lit up like a
pinball machine. He started jumping
around again. Then he called out, "Well,
bless my leotard, if it isn't Brother Bear.
He's coming to learn to dance on his tippy-
toes!"

Then Skuzz jumped right in front of the
door to the Center. He stood with his hands
on his hips and a nasty smile on his face. He
was blocking the cubs' way. Brother held on
to Sister's hand with his left hand and made
a fist with his right. He raised it at Skuzz.

"Better get out of our way," he said.

"Or what?" asked Skuzz.

"Or I'll rearrange your face," said Brother.

"Really?" gasped Skuzz in mock fear. Then his smile returned. "Is that something Madame Bearishnikov taught you in class? Face rearrangement? Is it anything like flower arrangement?"

Brother let go of Sister's hand. He made another fist. Just then Too-Tall came over and said sweetly, "Now, Skuzz, be a good little boy and let them in. If Brother gets into a fight, he might stub his little toe and ruin his big ballet career."

The whole gang broke into laughter. Skuzz stepped aside. With a deep bow and a sweep of his arm, he led the cubs into the Center.

Chapter 5

A Heavy Burden

Once inside, Sister said to Brother, "Don't let those guys get to you. There's nothing wrong with a boy coming to ballet class."

"Oh yeah?" said Brother. He looked around the large room. It was filled with girls in leotards and ballet shoes. They were all lined up doing warm-up exercises. "Then why am I the only boy here? Besides, I didn't come to class. I just walked *you* to class."

"Well, that's true," said Sister. "But when we leave, just walk past Too-Tall and his gang. Don't get into a fight with them. It won't do you any good."

Brother shrugged. It wasn't easy to take advice from his little sister. But this time she was right. "Okay," he said. "I'll do my best."

Just then Madame Bearishnikov noticed Brother. Her eyes lit up. "At last my prayers are answered!" she cried. She hurried over to Brother. Then she put her hands on his shoulders. "A fellow with the courage to be a dancer. Bravo! Bravo!"

She turned proudly to her students. "Behold, my darlings! At long last we have a male dancer—a strong, sturdy male dancer to do catches, lifts, and carries in the final scene of our great ballet recital!"

The students clapped loudly. A few yelled, "Yay, Brother!"

The room grew quiet. It seemed as if the students were waiting for Brother to make a speech about his love for ballet.

Brother swallowed hard. He cleared his

throat. "Well, Madame Bearishnikov," he said. "I . . . I don't . . . I didn't really . . . I mean, I'm not really . . ."

Madame Bearishnikov frowned. "Are you trying to say you didn't come here for ballet lessons?"

"Exactly," said Brother.

"And that you don't *want* to join our class today?"

Brother sighed. *Not today or in a million years,* he thought. "Right again," he said.

"So!" said the teacher.

Madame Bearishnikov looked Brother up and down again. But this time she was

not as friendly as before. Then she walked
all the way around him. She looked him up
and down a few more times. She began to
poke and pinch him. She acted as if he were
a chicken she was thinking of buying at the
supermarket.

"Hey, cut it out," Brother said under his
breath.

Madame Bearishnikov stood back and
looked Brother up and down once more. "I
was wrong, my darlings," she said. "This is
a puny chicken." She walked around him

again and frowned. "Yes. This is a puny chicken, with rubbery arms, wobbly legs, and muscles of Jell-O. Such a creature could never do the catches, lifts, and carries that a male dancer must do. Why, a strong wind would blow him away. Poof!"

"Oh, is that so?" said Brother. He couldn't let Madame Bearishnikov put him down like that in front of all the girl cubs. "Why don't you try me?"

"Hmm," said Madame Bearishnikov. "I suppose that's only fair. What do you think, class?"

The girl cubs all cried, "Yes!" Babs Bruno yelled, "Go for it, Brother!"

Brother looked around the room. He hoped to see Bonnie Brown smiling at him. But she wasn't even there. She must be in one of the other practice rooms, he thought. Too bad. Now she would miss him making the great ballet teacher look silly.

Madame Bearishnikov asked Brother to stand on a large mat in the middle of the room. "I think we should start with something easy. Let's try a simple catch," she said. "Sister, I want you to run to your brother and leap into his arms. All right?"

Sister nodded.

"Ready, Brother?" said the teacher.

"You bet!" said Brother. He put out his arms. Then he bent his knees.

Sister came running and leaped into Brother's arms. She hit him like a ton of bricks. Brother fell over backward. He hit the edge of the mat and landed right on his backside with a THUD. "Oof!" he gasped as Sister fell on top of him. "Ow!" cried Sister.

Everyone else laughed and laughed. They acted as if it were the funniest thing they had ever seen. Some of the girls laughed until they fell on the floor in tears.

"Now that's enough, all of you!" said Madame Bearishnikov. Brother picked himself up from the mat. The laughter died down. Brother could see that even Madame Bearishnikov was smiling. He blushed five shades of red.

"Well, Brother," the teacher went on, "I think you have given us all a good idea of what you can and can't do." There was more laughter from the girls. Madame Bearishnikov quieted them down. "Why don't you wait in the room to your right until your sister is done," she said.

Brother shuffled off into the next room. He closed the door behind him. Then he looked back through a little square window in the door. He could see the girls lining up in rows for exercises. Bonnie Brown came skipping in from another practice room. She looked extra pretty in her ballet clothes. Phew! Was Brother ever glad that Bonnie hadn't seen him fall on his backside!

Brother was wondering what he could do for the next hour. That was when he saw all sorts of barbells and exercise machines in the room. He was in a weight room! It

looked like fun. He could work out while he waited for Sister.

Brother went over to a barbell. He planted his feet firmly on the mat and lifted the barbell above his head. Then he set it down again. I'm no puny chicken, he thought. That Madame Bearishnikov just doesn't know what she's talking about!

Then Brother climbed up onto an exercise bike. He set it spinning with his powerful pedaling. Now he was sure that his

fall had just been bad luck. He was very strong. And he was in good shape!

The time flew by for Brother. When Sister finally poked her head through the door to call him, he felt tired but good. The two of them grabbed their jackets and hurried past Too-Tall and his gang.

"Look, Ma! I'm da-a-a-ancing! Look, Ma! . . ." yelled Too-Tall.

Brother and Sister headed home. Brother almost looked back over his shoulder at Bonnie Brown. But he forced himself not to. He knew he might see something he didn't want to see. He knew he might see Bonnie walking with that big jerk, Too-Tall Grizzly.

Chapter 6
A Sympathetic Ear

The next Saturday, Mama was about to take Sister to ballet class. But Brother offered to take her himself.

He offered again on the following Saturday, and on Tuesday and Thursday after school.

Ballet class was meeting more often now as the date of the recital got closer. Brother liked this because it gave him a chance to work out more often. His muscles were getting bigger and stronger by the day. He liked working out because it took his mind off his problems.

But he wished he didn't have to go to the Ballet Center to work out. Going there reminded him of his biggest problem of all—dancing. And on top of that, Bonnie Brown was always there and so was Too-Tall Grizzly. He was always hanging around outside the door. Seeing the two of them there made Brother very jealous.

Brother kept wondering if Bonnie had asked Too-Tall to the Spring Dance yet. Then, to make things even worse, he heard that the ballet recital and the Spring Dance would be held in the school gym on the very same day. They would both be held in the afternoon, first the recital and then the dance. That meant that after he watched Sister in the recital, he would have to slip away while all his friends stayed for the Spring Dance.

The Spring Dance started to feel like a big weight on Brother's shoulders. He knew he should do something about it. But what could he do except feel sorry for himself?

One day, while the ballet class was taking a break, Madame Bearishnikov came to see Brother in the weight room. She hadn't found a male dancer yet for the final scene of the ballet. It worried her a lot. But she hadn't given up on the idea of Brother becoming that dancer.

Brother put down the weights he held in each hand.

"Hmm," said Madame Bearishnikov. "It looks as if you are no longer the puny chicken."

"I never was," said Brother. "But I'm stronger than ever now."

"Yes, I can see that," said Madame

Bearishnikov. She came closer. "Are you sure you cannot help us with our final scene? It would just be a few simple lifts and carries. And the recital is still two weeks away. There would be plenty of time to practice."

Brother looked down at the mat. "I don't think so, Madame Bearishnikov."

"Perhaps you still think ballet is not for boys?" she asked.

"It isn't that, Madame Bearishnikov," answered Brother. "I've been watching your classes every now and then. It looks kind of fun. I would really like to help you. But I just don't think I can handle it right now. I have too much on my mind."

"Are you having a problem?" Madame Bearishnikov asked gently.

"You might say so," said Brother.

49

"A problem . . . of the heart?" said Madame Bearishnikov.

Brother sighed deeply. He dropped down to the mat and started doing push-ups.

"Ah, I see," said the ballet teacher. "Madame understands such problems. I will not press you."

Quietly, Madame Bearishnikov stepped out of the weight room. She left Brother Bear to his push-ups and his problems.

Chapter 7
The Thinking Place

The Spring Dance was less than a week away. Brother Bear finally decided it was time to visit his Thinking Place.

It was a rocky clearing in the woods not far from Bear Country School. Brother went there whenever he had a problem. He would sit and listen to the wind in the trees and think about his problem. He would usually find an answer.

He went there right after school. He sat and thought. He thought for a long time. His problem became clear.

Brother had to learn how to dance. Otherwise, Bonnie would go to the dance with Too-Tall Grizzly. And they would probably win the dance prize! Brother couldn't stand the thought of that.

But how could Brother learn to dance in less than a week? He thought back to his nightmare. It made him shudder. He thought and thought, but he could not figure out how to learn to dance in time for the big dance.

Brother was about to give up when a girl's voice said, "Brother?"

"Bonnie!" cried Brother. "What are you doing here?"

"I thought I would find you in your Sulking—I mean, Thinking—Place," said Bonnie.

"You did? Why?" said Brother.

Bonnie came over and sat down beside Brother. "Because I know how worried you are about the Spring Dance," she said. "And it's kind of my fault that you're so upset about it."

"How is it your fault?" said Brother. "Because you're going with Too-Tall?"

"I'm not going with Too-Tall," said Bonnie.

"But I thought—" said Brother.

"Oh, that was just a rumor I started. I thought it might get you to start dancing. Then I could ask *you* to the Spring Dance." Bonnie shrugged. "Well, it got you upset, but it didn't get you dancing. So I still can't ask you to the dance."

"I don't get it," said Brother. "You say you're not going to the dance with Too-Tall. And you're not going with me. So who *are* you going with?"

Bonnie smiled and shook her head. "You just don't get it, do you? I'm not going to the dance at all."

Now it was Brother's turn to shake his head. "Not going? What about the prize? You're such a great dancer. You could win! And you would win it for sure with Too-Tall. He's disgusting. But he's a great dancer."

"He is," said Bonnie. "But I'm not going *anywhere* with Too-Tall, especially not to the Spring Dance. He's much *too* disgusting."

When Brother heard that Bonnie wasn't gong to the dance with Too-Tall, he felt ten feet tall. But when it sank in that Bonnie wasn't going to the dance at all, he felt ten inches tall.

Brother began to feel guilty. Bonnie was going to stay home from the Spring Dance! She was going to give up the prize just so *his* feelings wouldn't be hurt! He felt terrible.

"But what are you going to do?" he asked Bonnie. "I mean the day of the dance?"

"Whatever you say," said Bonnie.

"What?" said Brother.

"We could go to a movie," she said. "Or we could go to the mall and just hang out. Whatever."

Wow, thought Brother. *She wants to hang out with me instead of go to the dance! She must really like me!*

Brother cleared his throat. He tried to think of something to say. Finally he said, "Gee, I don't know what to say."

"Just say everything is cool between us," said Bonnie. "And walk me home."

Brother said it. But it wasn't really true. As he and Bonnie walked home, Brother began to feel guilty again. It was all his fault that Bonnie would miss the dance. But what could he do about it? Only a miracle could make him a good dancer in time to go to the Spring Dance with her.

Chapter 8

A Good Trade

You can't stay sorry for someone forever. Even if it's your own brother. Sister had her own life to live. And for her, life was going great.

She was all set for the ballet recital. And it was less than a week away! That was great, but not perfect. Perfect would be if her mixed-up brother would help out with the ballet. She had the main role. All they needed was a boy cub to lift her and carry her at the end.

The truth was, she was getting a little tired of her gloomy brother. First he was upset because Bonnie was going to the dance. Now he was upset because she *wasn't* going to the dance. She couldn't keep up with him.

The two of them were heading for Madame Bearishnikov's. It was the last rehearsal before the recital. Sister was feeling so good she couldn't help showing it.

"Hey," she said, "want to see the new step Freddy and I have worked out for the new-step contest?"

"What?" said Brother. He came out of his trance.

"Never mind," said Sister.

"No, really. What is it?" said Brother.

"It's just that Freddy and I are going to win the new-step contest at the dance," said Sister.

"You sound very sure," said Brother.

"Well, why not? It's a great step. And Madame B. is a pretty good friend of mine," she added with a smile.

"What's she got to do with it?" said Brother.

"What's she got to do with it? She's only the judge of the whole Spring Dance!" said Sister.

"But she's a ballet dancer," said Brother.

"She's also a great pop dancer," said Sister. "Sometimes she shows us new steps after class. She's a very good teacher. Why, Madame B. could teach an old tree stump to dance!"

All of a sudden Sister had a great idea. If it worked, everything *would* be perfect. It would be perfect for her. And even better, it would be perfect for her dopey brother. She could hardly wait to get to ballet class to tell Madame Bearishnikov her idea.

Later that morning, Sister Bear and Bonnie Brown saw Madame Bearishnikov slip into the weight room during a break. They both stood by the door and listened. Madame Bearishnikov was talking to Brother, who was working out on the exercise bike.

"May I talk with you a minute, Brother?" asked the teacher.

"Sure," said Brother. He hopped down from the bike. "What can I do for you, Madame Bearishnikov?" Brother asked.

"You can make a trade with me," said the teacher.

"A trade? Do you collect baseball cards?"

Madame Bearishnikov laughed. "No, Brother. I'm talking about another kind of trade. This is where I do something to help you if you do something to help me."

"What do I have to do?" asked Brother.

"Help us with our ballet recital. It will be a great success if you are in it," said Madame Bearishnikov.

Brother frowned.

"Don't you want to know what *I* will do for *you?*" the teacher asked.

"I guess so. What is it?" said Brother.

"I'll teach you to be a pretty good pop dancer in time for the Spring Dance," said Madame Bearishnikov.

Brother's eyes opened wide. "Could you really do that?" he asked.

"Sure," said Madame Bearishnikov. "I'm an expert. And it would just be you and me.

No one else would be watching."

That was all Brother needed to hear. "I'll do it!" he said.

When Sister and Bonnie heard Brother agree to the trade, they whispered "Yay!" and high-fived.

"Now," said Madame Bearishnikov, "you will need to come to the Center every day after school to practice. You will learn to do lifts, catches, and carries with Sister and Bonnie for half an hour.

"Then you and I will practice pop dancing for another half an hour. But I don't want you falling behind in your schoolwork. Is that understood?"

"No problem," said Brother. He was ready to do anything in order to go with Bonnie to the Spring Dance. "But what about Sister and Bonnie?" he asked. "Do they have time for this?"

Madame Bearishnikov smiled. She looked back toward the main practice room. She knew that Sister and Bonnie were probably listening behind the door. "Oh, don't worry about them," she said. "I'm sure I can talk them into it. Now for your first lesson. Can you dance at all?"

"A little," said Brother. "I can do the Box Step."

"That's a beginning, at least," said Madame Bearishnikov. Then she walked over to Brother. "Now, put your arms around me and we shall start. No! Don't hold me as if I am a cream puff. Hold me as if I am the steering wheel of a powerful racing car!"

Behind the door, Sister and Bonnie high-fived again.

Chapter 9
Too-Tall's Ballet Lesson

Brother's first ballet practice was set for the next day after school. The three cubs walked together to the mall. The girls noticed that Brother had real bounce to his step. He was even whistling a popular dance tune.

"Hey, what's gotten into you?" asked Bonnie. Of course, she and Sister knew what had gotten into him. He was happy because he was finally going to learn to dance. But he hadn't told them yet. So they were playing it cool.

"Oh, nothing much," said Brother

cheerfully. "By the way, did I tell you two that I'm taking dance lessons?"

"No!" said the girls. They winked at each other. "Who is your teacher?" asked Sister.

"Madame Bearishnikov," said Brother.

"You don't say!" said Bonnie.

"Sure," said Brother. "And I'm going to be in your ballet recital."

"What do you mean?" asked Sister. She was trying not to giggle.

"Madame B. and I made a deal. You don't think I would agree to be in the recital for nothing, do you?"

Sister and Bonnie looked at one another. "I guess not," they both said.

"Anyway," Brother said, "I have a lesson right after ballet practice. That means I won't be able to walk home with you."

"Couldn't we stay and watch?" asked Bonnie. Sister made a face at her. Then she elbowed her in the ribs.

"No way," said Brother. "Nobody watches."

"Then Madame B. will have to close her eyes while she's teaching you," teased Bonnie.

"Ha-ha, very funny," said Brother.

"We could hang out in the main practice room and wait for you," said Sister.

"I guess that would be all right," said Brother. "But no peeking. Promise?"

"Promise!" said the girls.

Brother looked over at Bonnie. She looked back at him with a big smile on her face.

That smile said everything. It said how proud she was of him. It said she was proud of him for having the courage to learn to dance. And it said how glad she was that they could go to the Spring Dance together after all.

Brother gave Bonnie a big smile back.

The cubs kept their extra practices a secret. It was nice to come to the Ballet Center without having to put up with Too-Tall and his gang.

The ballet practice went very well. Brother was very fit and strong now from his workout program. And he had no trouble learning the lifts and catches. For those he just stood still. The carries were a little harder because he had to learn to move like a ballet dancer. But he knew he would be fine with a little more practice.

After practice Sister and Bonnie went into the next room so that Brother could have his popular-dancing lesson in private. But Brother was taking no chances. He asked Madame Bearishnikov to take down an exercise poster from the wall and hang it over the little square window in the door.

The lesson went just as well as the ballet practice. Madame Bearishnikov was a good teacher. When they were finished, Brother knew he could do the Grunge better than some cubs who had been doing it all spring.

"Tomorrow I'll teach you the Slew-Foot," said Madame Bearishnikov as she and Brother went into the main room.

Brother, Sister, and Bonnie said good-bye to Madame Bearishnikov and headed for the front door. Bonnie started to open it but quickly closed it again. "Oh no," she said. "It's Too-Tall and his gang. How did they find out so fast that we were here?"

"Oh, they have spies everywhere," said Sister. "One of them probably saw us go into the Center earlier. Then he rushed off to tell the whole gang."

"Don't worry about them," said Brother. "We know that all they will do is jump around and yell, 'Look, Ma! We're da-a-a-ancin'!' Just pretend not to notice them."

But what the cubs didn't know was that

this time Too-Tall was out to get Brother Bear. He had been sure that Bonnie was going to invite him to the dance. But the dance was just a few days away. And she hadn't said anything to him.

Too-Tall was starting to lose patience. He decided that now was the time to make a move on Bonnie. If Brother didn't like it . . . well, so much the better.

As the cubs left the Center, Too-Tall came stomping up to them. He had an angry look on his face. Vinnie, Skuzz, and Smirk were right behind him. "Hey, beautiful," he said, and winked at Bonnie. "Why are you hanging around with this little twerp? Everyone knows it's me you like. And since you're going to the dance with me, let's get it on right now. Come on, baby, I'll show you how to do the Snake."

Too-Tall reached for Bonnie. But before

he could touch her, Brother grabbed his arm. Too-Tall glared at Brother. He couldn't figure out why Brother wasn't afraid of him.

The weeks of training had made Brother super strong. By now even his muscles had muscles. "Better yet, Too-Tall," he said, "*I'll* show *you* how to do the Snake."

Quick as lightning, Brother had Too-Tall in a wrestling hold that twisted him up like

a pretzel. Too-Tall didn't even have time to yell "Stop!" Brother lifted him high with a perfect ballet lift. Then he hauled him over to a Dumpster with a perfect ballet carry and dropped him in.

Brother dusted off his hands and turned to Bonnie and Sister. "Ladies, shall we . . . move on?" He gave a little ballet kick. Then he offered Sister one arm and Bonnie the other. Off they strolled down the mall.

Vinnie, Skuzz, and Smirk were left with their mouths hanging open. All they could do was stand there staring after the cubs.

"You'll pay for this!" screamed Too-Tall. He was stuck inside the filthy Dumpster. "Don't just stand there, you creeps!" he yelled to his gang. "Get me outta here!"

Chapter 10
Dance Till You Drop

Madame Bearishnikov's ballet recital was a big hit. The audience loved Sister Bear. They clapped extra loudly for her solo number. The last piece was the high point of the show. Brother Bear performed every catch, lift, and carry as if he had been practicing all spring. The final curtain came down to thunderous applause. The dancers were brought back for five curtain calls.

As soon as the show was over, a stage crew started to clear the gym for the Spring Dance. Cubs stood around and talked at one end of the gym. Brother, Bonnie, and Sister

were still in their ballet costumes. Everyone was there—Freddy, Lizzy Bruin, Barry Bruin, Babs Bruno, Queenie, Skuzz, Smirk, and Vinnie.

Well, almost everyone. Too-Tall wasn't there. He was in the boys' locker room. He had a big job to do. And he knew that he had no time to lose.

Any minute now Brother would come to his locker to change for the dance. Too-Tall knew just which locker was Brother's. He also knew that Brother never locked it.

Quickly Too-Tall reached into his pocket

and took out a small box. He shook its contents onto something hanging in Brother's locker. Just as Too-Tall was closing the door he heard someone walk into the locker room. It was Brother! Had he seen him closing the locker?

Too-Tall scooted around the corner and hid in the shower room. He pressed himself flat up against the cool wall. He could hear Brother dressing and happily humming to himself. Good! He hadn't been seen! Too-Tall had to stop himself from laughing out loud.

In the meantime, cubs had started to arrive for the dance. Queenie had come to the dance with Too-Tall. But now she couldn't find him. She looked high and low for him.

"Did you lose something?" asked Skuzz.

"Yeah, Too-Tall," said Queenie. "Where is he?"

"He's on important business," said Skuzz. "Stay cool. He'll be back in a minute."

The sound of loud clapping rang out as Brother stepped onto the dance floor with Bonnie on his arm. Word had gotten around about Too-Tall and the Dumpster. Brother was a hero.

"Imagine, clapping for that little creep," said Too-Tall. "They'll change their tune pretty soon," he added. Then he smiled wickedly.

"Oh, there you are," said Queenie to Too-Tall. "Come on. We have to start dancing if we're going to win the contest."

"We have time for that. Let's just watch for a while," said Too-Tall. Queenie was puzzled.

The dance was now in full swing. The

cubs were dancing like there was no tomorrow. Sister and Freddy were doing the Grunge. Babs Bruno and Skuzz were doing the Slew-Foot. Madame Bearishnikov was watching the dancers. She took notes as she walked among them.

"Where did you disappear to before?" Queenie asked Too-Tall. "I thought maybe you dumped me the way a certain someone dumped you in the mall Dumpster."

"I was busy taking care of that certain someone," said Too-Tall. "There he is now. He's starting to dance with that two-timing Bonnie. Just watch this."

Everyone was watching Brother and Bonnie. Bonnie Brown was the best dancer on the floor. As for Brother—no one had ever seen him dance before. And he was doing fine! Madame Bearishnikov smiled proudly.

But all of a sudden a strange look came over Brother's face. He stopped dancing and stood still. Still as a statue.

Oh no! thought Bonnie. Was Brother's fear of dancing coming back? Not *now!*

Madame Bearishnikov looked over at them. Bonnie saw her and started dancing up a storm. She hoped the teacher would look at her instead of Brother.

Too-Tall turned to Queenie and grinned. "Now watch this," he said.

"What's happening?" asked Queenie.

"What's happening? I'll tell you what's happening—*I put itching powder in Brother's shorts!*"

Brother still had a strange look on his face. But he wasn't standing still. Every part of his body was moving. Especially the part wearing shorts. Brother had become a wildly wiggling, twitching, twisting, humongous super-dancer.

All the other cubs, even Bonnie, stopped to watch. No one could believe what they saw. Brother just kept twisting and turning.

The crowd started to clap loudly. As the clapping got louder and louder, Brother's dance got wilder and wilder. Finally he dropped exhausted to the floor.

"Your attention, please!" said Madame Bearishnikov. "I am most proud to announce that, for his great performance, Brother Bear has won the prize for Most Original Step! And for her great solo, Bonnie Brown has won the prize for Best Dancer!"

Madame Bearishnikov let the clapping
go on for a while. Then she asked the cubs
to quiet down. She looked down at Brother,

who was still on the floor. "By the way," she said. "What is the name of that most original new dance of yours?"

Brother was so out of breath he could hardly talk. He pulled Bonnie down and whispered something in her ear. Bonnie looked a bit puzzled when she heard the name of the dance.

But the next thing Brother did was *really* a puzzle. He leaped up and raced off the dance floor toward the boys' locker room.

That dance of Brother's was quite a performance. To this day, they still talk about it in Bear Country. And even though Brother became a very good dancer, he never again danced the way he did that afternoon. Only a small number of his friends—and enemies—know what came over Brother that day.

So, why did Brother race off the dance floor? Because he had to get out of those itchy shorts and into a nice cool shower!

And what did Brother name his prize-winning new dance? You can see the name written on the trophy sitting in the showcase outside the principal's office.

He named it *The Itch*.

Stan and Jan Berenstain began writing and illustrating books for children in the early 1960s, when their two young sons were beginning to read. That marked the start of the best-selling Berenstain Bears series. Now, with more than 95 books in print, videos, television shows, and even a Berenstain Bears theme park, it's hard to tell where the Bears end and the Berenstains begin!

Stan and Jan make their home in Bucks County, Pennsylvania, and plan on writing and illustrating many more books for children, especially for their four grandchildren, who keep them well in touch with the kids of today.